Joseph P. Thompson, Union League Club

Revolution Against Free Government not a Right but a Crime

an address by Joseph P. Thompson delivered before the Union League

Club, and published at their request - Vol. 1

Joseph P. Thompson, Union League Club

Revolution Against Free Government not a Right but a Crime
*an address by Joseph P. Thompson delivered before the Union League Club, and
published at their request - Vol. 1*

ISBN/EAN: 9783337235475

Printed in Europe, USA, Canada, Australia, Japan

Cover: Foto ©Andreas Hilbeck / pixelio.de

More available books at **www.hansebooks.com**

REVOLUTION

AGAINST

FREE GOVERNMENT

NOT A RIGHT BUT A CRIME.

———•••———

AN ADDRESS

BY

JOSEPH P. THOMPSON, D. D.,

DELIVERED BEFORE

THE UNION LEAGUE CLUB,

AND PUBLISHED AT THEIR REQUEST.

CLUB·HOUSE, UNION SQUARE,

No. 26 East Seventeenth St.

1864.

UNION LEAGUE CLUB,

26 EAST SEVENTEENTH STREET, *March* 15, 1864.

REV. JOSEPH P. THOMPSON, D.D.:

MY DEAR SIR:—It gives me great pleasure to be the medium of communicating to you the action of the Union League Club, at their last
monthly meeting, after the delivery of your eloquent address.

The following resolutions were unanimously adopted:

"*Resolved*, That the thanks of the Union League Club be tendered to
"the Rev. Joseph P. Thompson, D.D., for his lucid and eloquent exposition
"of the rights of man and the principles of Free Governments, and of the
"turpitude of armed rebellion against a Government so just and beneficent
"as that under which we live.

"*Resolved*, That the Rev. Dr. Thompson be requested by the Secretary
"to furnish the Club with a copy of his discourse, for publication by the
"Club."

Indulging the hope, in common with those who enjoyed the privilege
of hearing your address, that the request of the Club will be granted,

I am, Rev. and dear Sir,

Yours truly,

OTIS D. SWAN, *Secretary.*

———

32 WEST THIRTY-SIXTH STREET, *March* 21, 1864.

MR. OTIS D. SWAN, *Secretary Union League Club:*

DEAR SIR:—Your favor of the 15th, communicating the request of the
Union League Club for the publication of my address on Revolution, is
gratefully acknowledged. I shall be happy to place the manuscript at
their disposal as soon as I can prepare it for the press. Be pleased to
express to the Club my thanks for their courteous reception and their
complimentary resolution; and accept for yourself my acknowledgment
of the handsome manner in which you have conveyed to me their action.

I am, dear Sir,

Very respectfully,

JOS. P. THOMPSON.

REVOLUTION AGAINST FREE GOVERNMENT NOT A RIGHT BUT A CRIME.

THE QUESTION FUNDAMENTAL.

THE war is schooling the nation in the principles that must hereafter secure the peaccable administration of its affairs. A government based upon the broadest doctrine of human rights, and framed in the soundest principles of political philosophy, is assailed not in its methods or measures, but at its foundation. The mine of the conspirators was sprung under the arches upon which the whole fabric rests, and the ground trembles and the walls and pillars vibrate with the concussion. To reassure ourselves that the Constitution, the Union, the Government will stand, we must go down and explore the foundations—to see whether any accepted principle has been dislodged; any pillar shaken out of place; any arch or beam is cracked and ready to fall. The scrutiny may be anxious and severe; but the process is salutary and the result certain. It is to-day as Richard Hooker wrote two centuries ago : "The stateliness of houses, the goodliness of trees, when we behold them, delighteth the eye : but that foundation which beareth up the one, that root which ministereth unto the other nourishment and life, is in the bosom of the earth concealed ; and if there be at any time occasion to search into it, such labor is then more necessary than pleasant, both to them which undertake it and for the lookers-on. In like manner, the use and benefit of good laws, all that live under them may enjoy with delight and comfort; albeit the grounds and first original causes from which they have sprung be unknown, as to the greatest part of men they are. But when they who withdraw their obedience, pretend that the laws which they should obey are corrupt and vicious; for better examination of their quality, it behooveth the very foundation and root, the highest wellspring and fountain of them, to be discovered. Which, because we are not oftentimes accustomed to do, when we do it, the pains we take are more needful a great deal than acceptable."*

Rather would I say they are then acceptable because they are needful. Needful all the pains and cost of war; needful all the toil of thought, by speech and pen interpreting the lessons of the war and shaping its results; needful that brain and blood should together work out the great issue of the conflict, by force of ideas no less than by the victory of the sword. For, that which we must needs determine now, is not only that this Free Government has the physical strength to stand, but that it stands upon what is itself settled and stable, because right and true. This is the issue raised by the rebellion, which would displace Liberty for Slavery as the cornerstone of political society, and would subvert the Republic by pleading against it that very right of revolution by which we won our place as a nation.

CALHOUN THE AUTHOR OF THE REBELLION.

This issue of ideas—like every conflict of principle—is historical. Hardly was American independence

* Eccl. Polity, B. i. c. 1.

achieved, when there began to appear symptoms of reaction against republican institutions; and while schemes for reviving an aristocracy were nipped in the bud, a system of social despotism was suffered to root itself in a soil consecrated to liberty. Jefferson tells us that when the air breathed suspicions of monarchists in the first cabinet, Washington said to him " that he considered our Constitution an experiment on the practicability of republican government, and with what dose of liberty man could be trusted for his own good; that he was determined the experiment should have a fair trial, and would lose the last drop of his blood in support of it."*

Scarce half a century had elapsed when the doctrine that liberty is an inalienable birthright of man from the Creator, was denounced in the Senate of the United States as " the most false and dangerous of all political errors." In his speech of June 27, 1848, on the Oregon Bill, Mr. Calhoun declared his conviction of the folly and danger of "admitting so great an error to have a place in our Declaration of Independence," and went so far as to forebode the destruction of our Union and system of government as the legitimate result of this grave fundamental error.† To counteract what Washington

---

* Jefferson's Works, vi. 288.

† " Let me say, Senators, if our Union and system of government are doomed to perish, and we to share the fate of so many great people who have gone before us, the historian who, in some future day, may record the events ending in so calamitous a result, will devote his first chapter to the ordinance of 1787, lauded as it and its authors have been, as the first of that series which led to it. His next chapter will be devoted to the Missouri Compromise, and the next to the present agitation. * * * If he should possess a philosophical turn of mind, and be disposed to look to more remote and recondite causes, he will trace it to a proposition which originated in a hypothetical truism, but which, as now expressed and now understood, is the most false and dangerous of all political errors." Mr.

styled a large dose of liberty, Calhoun and his school of practitioners began to experiment with what dose of Slavery a republican people could be plied without wincing or retching. And with every dose the threat was, Take this or die;—Slave-rule or Dissolution.

. Twenty-five years ago this rebellion was distinctly proclaimed by Calhoun in the Senate. "God forbid," said he, "I should ever deny the glorious right of rebellion and revolution. Should corruption and oppression become intolerable, and not otherwise be thrown off—if liberty must perish, or the government be overthrown, I would not hesitate, at the hazard of life, to resort to revolution, and to tear down a corrupt government that could neither be reformed nor borne by freemen."* This sounds like the assertion of a grand right of oppressed humanity; a heroic self-sacrifice for liberty, an echo of the very Declaration he had despised; but when we inquire what is the liberty for which Calhoun would attempt a revolution, we find it the liberty to have property in man, without encroachment from Northern opinion or restriction from territorial legislation. When we ask what are the oppressions against which he would revolt, he tells us that all attempts to disturb or question the right to hold slaves as property, "with the view to its subversion, are direct and dangerous outrages;" and he appeals to the South to resist such outrages by force of arms.†

Calhoun then denounces the popular saying, "all men are born free and equal," and adds that in the Declaration of Independence, "the form of expression, though less dangerous, *is not less erroneous.*" (Works, iv. 506-8.)

* Works, ii. 615. Speech of Jan. 5th on Michigan.

† Vol. iv. 529 and vol. iii. 443.

In his speech of Aug. 12, 1849, upon the Missouri Compromise Line, Mr. Calhoun denounced the North because of the abolition agitation, predicted the triumph of abolitionism in some future Presidential election,

Here, then, we may study the rebellion in its root and principle. The whole case lies in this nutshell—Washington willing to shed the last drop of his blood for the National Constitution as an instrument of freedom, Calhoun ready to overthrow that Constitution by rebellion unless he could use it, without restraint or protest, for the defence and conservation of human slavery.

For a time, Liberty itself trembled within the sacred ark to which the fathers had committed it. For, in the and declared that "nothing short of the united and fixed determination of the South to maintain her rights at every hazard, could stop it."

"If I am right," said he, "the South is under solemn obligation, both to herself and to the rest of the Union, to rally and take the remedy in her own hands, and that speedily, as the only possible mode to bring the North to pause and reflect on consequences, if, indeed, it be not already too late for that; and if, unfortunately, it should prove to be so, to save herself." (iv. p. 530.)

In his speech on the Slavery Question, March 4th, 1850, Mr. Calhoun insisted that the North should appease the South by opening new territory to slave emigration, by ceasing to agitate the slave question, and by so amending the Constitution that the South could have the power of protecting herself against the preponderance of Northern States. Such, in his view, would be a just settlement of sectional questions. But, said he, "if you who represent the stronger portion cannot agree to settle them on the broad principle of justice and duty, say so; and let the States we both represent agree to separate and part in peace. If you are unwilling we should part in peace, tell us so, and we shall know what to do, when you reduce the question to submission or resistance." (Works, iv. 573.)

In his speech of Dec. 27, 1837, upon the Rights of the States, Mr. Calhoun distinctly avowed the right of State rebellion against the General Government.

"The only remedy is in the States' Rights doctrines; and, if those who profess them in slaveholding States do not rally on them as their political creed, and organize as a party against the fanatics, in order to put them down, the South and West will be compelled to take the remedy into their own hands. They will then stand justified in the sight of God and man; and what, in that event, will follow, no mortal can anticipate." (Vol. iii. 155.)

The South "had no fears for herself. She was full of resources, and would, he trusted, be prepared to meet the crisis whenever forced on her by the injustice or insults of the other portion of the Union." (iii. 195.)

13*

rising flood of Southern domination, Liberty, as Coleridge said of Burke, was "shut up, as it were, in a Noah's ark, with very few men. and a great many beasts." The danger was that brute force and bloody threats would gain the mastery over liberty and law, over justice and virtue. Restrained at last in its encroachments upon the Constitution, the Slave-power broke forth, as Calhoun had threatened, in insurrection against the Constitution and the Union, and taking their cue from the master-spirit of

---

In his speech on the Abolition Petitions, March 9, 1836, Mr. Calhoun insisted that the Senate should deny a hearing to such petitions.

" But if," said he, "instead of closing the door—if, instead of denying all jurisdiction and all interference in this question, the doors of Congress are to be thrown open; and if we are to be exposed here, in the heart of the Union, to endless attacks on our rights, our character, and our institutions; if the other States are to stand and look on without attempting to suppress these attacks originating within their borders. and, finally, if this is to be our fixed and permanent condition, as members of this Confederacy. we will then be compelled to turn our eyes on ourselves. Come what will, should it cost every drop of blood, and every cent of property, we must defend ourselves; and if compelled, we would stand justified by all laws, human and divine." (ii. 488.)

In his speech on State Rights, Feb. 26, 1833, Mr. C. said, " the right of the States to judge of the extent of their reserved powers stands on the most solid foundation, and is good against every department of the General Government; and the judiciary is as much excluded from an interference with the reserved powers as the legislative or executive departments." (Vol. ii. 298.)

In his speech of April 12, 1836, on " Suppressing Incendiary Publications," Mr. Calhoun took the ground that in matters concerning State institutions and policy. the laws of the General Government must yield to State laws:—" the low must yield to the high; the convenient to the necessary ; mere accommodation to safety and security." He warns the Senate that they will become abettors of Abolitionists.

"Should such be your decision, by refusing to pass this bill. I shall say to the people of the South, Look to yourselves—you have nothing to hope from others. But I must tell the Senate, be your decision what it may. the South will never abandon the principles of this bill. If you refuse co-operation with our laws, and conflict should ensue between yours and ours, the Southern States will never yield to the superiority of yours. We have a remedy in our hands. which in such event we shall not fail to apply.

nullification, the leaders of the rebellion assert before the world their right of revolution, pleading the precedent of our national origin. The declaration lately put forth by the Congress at Richmond avows that the protection of slave property was the motive of the rebellion; that the preservation of the relations of labor and capital created by Slavery is the object of the Rebel Confederacy; for which, says the Congress, "we fell back upon the right for which the colonies maintained the war of the Revo-

We have high authority for asserting that, in such cases, 'State interposition is the rightful remedy'—a doctrine first announced by Jefferson—adopted by the patriotic and republican State of Kentucky, by a solemn resolution, in '98, and finally carried out into successful practice on a recent occasion, ever to be remembered, by the gallant State which I in part have the honor to represent. In this well-tested and efficient remedy, sustained by the principles developed in the report, and asserted in this bill, the slaveholding States have an ample protection. Let it be fixed—let it be riveted in every Southern mind—that the laws of the slaveholding States for the protection of their domestic institutions are paramount to the laws of the General Government in regulation of commerce and the mail; that the latter must yield to the former in the event of conflict; and that if the Government should refuse to yield, the States have a right to interpose, and we are safe. With these principles, nothing but concert would be wanting to bid defiance to the movements of the abolitionists, whether at home or abroad; and to place our domestic institutions, and with them our security and peace, under our own protection, and beyond the reach of danger." (Vol. ii. 532, 533.)

In his Remarks on the Slave Question, Feb. 19, 1847, Mr. Calhoun, insisting upon the right of Southerners "to emigrate with their [slave] property to the territories of the United States," uttered this threat:

" Well, sir, what if the decision of this body shall deny to us this high constitutional right, not the less clear because deduced from the entire body of the instrument, and the nature of the subject to which it relates, instead of being specially provided for? What then? I will not undertake to decide. It is a question for our constituents, the slaveholding States—a solemn and a grave question. If the decision should be adverse, I trust and do believe that they will take under solemn consideration what they ought to do. I give no advice. It would be hazardous and dangerous for me to do so. But I may speak as an individual member of that section of the Union. There is my family and connections; there I drew my first breath; there are all my hopes. I am a planter—a cotton

lution, and which our heroic forefathers asserted to be
clear and inalienable."*

EARL RUSSELL'S SOPHISM.

This plea finds favor in high quarters abroad; and its
speciousness has served to cover the intrinsic atrocity of
the Southern rebellion. Earl Russell, in his speech at
Blairgowrie, on the 26th of September, 1863, alluded in
these terms to political rebellion as an established precedent in the English theory of the State. He says of Mr.
Sumner: "I cannot but wonder that this man, the offspring of three, as we are of two rebellions, should be
speaking like the Czar of Russia or Louis XIV. of the
dreadful guilt of the crime of rebellion. I recollect that
we rebelled against Charles I., against James II., and
that the people of New England, not content with these,
rebelled against George III. I do not say now whether
all these were justifiable or wrong. I do not say whether
the rebellion of the Southern States is a justifiable insurrection—whether it is a great fact or a great crime—but

planter. I am a southern man and a slaveholder—a kind and a merciful
one, I trust—and none the worse for being a slaveholder. I say, for one,
I would rather meet any extremity upon earth than give up one inch of
our equality—one inch of what belongs to us as members of this great republic! What! acknowledged inferiority! The surrender of life is nothing
to sinking down into acknowledged inferiority. (iv. 347.)

"The day that the balance between the slaveholding States and the
non-slaveholding States is destroyed, is a day that will not be far removed
from political revolution, anarchy, civil war, and wide-spread disaster."
(Vol. iii. 343.)

* "Compelled by a long series of oppressive and tyrannical acts, culmi-
nating at last in the selection of a President and Vice-President by a party
confessedly sectional, and hostile to the South and her institutions, these
States withdrew from the former Union, and formed a new Confederate
alliance, as an independent Government, based on the proper relations of
labor and capital.

"This step was taken reluctantly, by constraint, and after the exhaus-
tion of every measure that was likely to secure us from interference with

I state the mere fact, that a rebellion is not in itself a crime of so deep a dye as to cause us to renounce our relations with people guilty of rebellion."

This seemed so clever a hit at Mr. Sumner that Lord John's auditors accepted it with much applause, as the end of argument. Yet it is simply a play upon words—and begs the question as to principles. Indeed, nothing could be more shallow than the assumption upon which Earl Russell's reasoning rests, and nothing more hostile to the well-being of society than the conclusion toward which it points. The right of armed resistance to government—call it rebellion or revolution—is not a naked abstract right, lodged within the political structure as a corrective power, to be invoked at pleasure; it is at best a qualified and conditional right, and can exist only in extreme cases of justifying circumstances. We cannot say, "A rebellion is a rebellion;" or, "Our fathers rebelled, therefore may we;" for, the conditions failing, that which was made to them a right may be in us a crime.

MR. JEFFERSON'S FALLACIES.

The loose popular notion that revolution is a fixed right in society may be traced to a fallacy of Mr. Jefferson, which is so transparent that it needs only to be stated to refute itself. "The earth," says Jefferson, "belongs always to the living generation; they may manage it, then, and what proceeds from it, as they please, during

our property, equality in the Union, or exemption from submission to an alien government. The Southern States claimed only the unrestricted enjoyment of the rights guaranteed by the Constitution. Finding, by painful and protracted experience, that this was persistently denied, we determined to separate from those enemies, who had manifested the inclination and ability to impoverish and destroy us; we fell back upon the right for which the colonies maintained the war of the Revolution, and which our heroic forefathers asserted to be clear and inalienable."

their usufruct. They are masters, too, of their own persons, and consequently may govern them as they please. But persons and property make the sum of the objects of government. The constitution and the laws of their predecessors are extinguished then, in their natural course, with those whose will gave them being. This [will] could preserve that being till it ceased to be itself, and no longer. Every constitution, then, and every law, naturally expires at the end of thirty-four years. If it be enforced longer, it is an act of force, and not of right."*

Perhaps it is enough to say of this astounding theory, that it was written in Paris, in 1789; it is French Directory liberty, the liberty of the barricade supported by the guillotine, not Anglo-Saxon liberty, founded in institutions and girt about with law. The theory contains a threefold fallacy. 1. It ignores the fact that men of different generations are always mingled together, contemporaneously profiting by each other's labors; so that it is impossible to mark the term where one generation begins and another ends. Vital statistics have averaged this at thirty-three years; but the curtain does not fall upon the stage of life three times in a century, that the earth may be cleared of one generation and another may appear. Generations do not march on and off the stage in platoons; men are born and grow; and hence, as Sir James Mackintosh has aptly said, "governments are not made, but grow."

2. Again, Jefferson's theory makes no account of principles as entering into the constitution of society and of government—*ethical* principles, that have a permanent life, and that one generation plants with toil and blood for its successors. No after generation has a right to dis-

* Works, vol. iii. 106, Letter to Madison.

card these, and so deprive its posterity of the fruits of the Past. Under no pretext can we surrender the rights of free speech, a free press, a free conscience, which we hold as a heritage from the Past in trust for the Future.

3. And hence, thirdly, the theory overlooks the fact that human society is organic, and exists in continuity, with certain great, uniform, transmissible and indefeasible interests.

Yet so possessed was Mr. Jefferson with his Parisian theory, that he would even provide for periodical revolution as a healthy agitation of society. Alluding to the Massachusetts insurrection, he says : " The late rebellion in Massachusetts has given more alarm than I think it should have done. Calculate that one rebellion in thirteen States, in the course of eleven years, is but one for each State in a century and a half. No country should be so long without a revolution."* And to carry out these notions in practice, Jefferson would provide in the social organism itself that " each generation, at intervals of twenty years, should solemnly revise its government, or choose for itself the form of government it believes most promotive of its own happiness;" since, without this periodical repairing of the whole political structure, " men will go on in the endless circle of oppression, rebellion, and reformation."

But Mr. Jefferson's philosophy of rebellion is as fallacious as are Earl Russell's historical parallels. That state of affairs upon which the right of revolution is grounded, being itself conditional, may not only fail to recur in every thirty, or hundred, or two hundred years —but, through the improved organization of political society, may cease ever again to be possible: and its justifying

* Vol. ii. 331.

conditions being precluded by the social constitution itself, the right would thenceforth determine, and could not be revived by appeals to precedent.

THE QUESTION DEFINED.

Every plea for revolution assumes the improvableness of human society; it is for bettering man's condition. But how much is society bettered, if, by the very theory of its improvement, it must always be liable to a violent overturning? if the background of the social order is not reason and moral right, but physical force? if the state, when founded in sound ethical principles, and constituted for the highest welfare of society, must still harbor within its bosom the explosive force of revolution? For to assert a permanent right of revolution against any and every form of political organization, is practically to govern human society by force, or by dread of force, till the end of time. Yet progressive revolutionists, of whatever creed, believe in the perfectibility of human society, and make the perfection of the social state their ultimate end. This I too accept, both as a political creed and as a practical aim; and in denying any further right of revolution under a specific form of political organization, I do but declare a broader faith in certain ultimate truths of political ethics, and in certain ultimate facts in the constitution of society. Revolution, or a series of revolutions, may lead to the recognition of these truths and the establishment of these facts in the political structure. But once that point is reached, and political society is distinctly and fairly established upon these facts and truths, and for these ends, then, in an age when knowledge and Christianity have free play, the permanence of moral causes influencing society will so far secure the well-ordering of the state, that its overthrow by violence can never become a right and a duty; but to attempt this must always be a wrong and a crime.

In other words, when a community has reached that high state of political organization in which these things are secured—*to wit*, A free popular government with all its appropriate institutions (to be hereafter defined), and a constitution duly regulating the administration of that government, and itself amendable by the people, then, by virtue of those moral causes which in such an organization will essentially secure the well-ordering of the state, the right of revolution ceases from that community, and an armed uprising against such a free, popular, constitutional government, being necessarily without justifying conditions, can never become rightful, but must be always and simply a crime.

The proposition in this general form may startle some by its novelty, and others by the breadth and the boldness of its assertion. It runs athwart traditions and prejudices derived from our own revolutionary epoch; yet it harmonizes with the Declaration of Independence. It contradicts that style of Fourth-of-July declamation which has gone to seed in this Southern rebellion; but it is the logical sequence of the true doctrine of revolution.

To clothe it in a concrete form: We who are of English blood, and heirs of English liberty, did rebel and rightfully rebel against Charles I.; we rebelled again, and rightfully, against James II.; and again the third time we rebelled rightfully against George III. But did we thereby establish the law of an indefinite series of rebellions, justified by precedent, and to recur at intervals, as a condition of progress for the Anglo-Saxon race? True, each of the first two rebellions was a justifying precedent for that which came after; yet each, in proportion to the permanent value of its own gains, lessened the area of rightful revolution; and our revolution of 1776, with its final and perfect result in the Constitution of 1789, swept over every remaining point of revolutionary right upon this soil; so that, instead of here establishing the right of revolution as an article of our political faith, and a sacred precedent for after ages, it really exhausted that right by its own success. Our fathers fought to establish not the right of revolution, but the rights of man, and a government that should conserve those rights, and should therefore stand till the end of time.

STABILITY OF GOVERNMENT.

Now, the well-being of political society requires *stability in government*, no less than freedom of individual life and of social progress under that government. Mr. J. Stuart Mill—than whom there is none abler upon such a theme—lays down as a condition of permanent political society, "the existence, in some form or other, of the feeling of allegiance or loyalty. This feeling may vary in its objects, and is not confined to any particular form of government; but whether in a democracy or in a monarchy, its essence is always the same; viz. : that there be in the constitution of the state *something* which is settled, something permanent, and not to be called in question; something which, by general agreement, has a right to be where it is, and to be secure against disturbance, whatever else may change. In all political societies which have had a durable existence, there has been some

fixed point; something which men agreed in holding
sacred; which it might or might not be lawful to contest
in theory, but which no one could either fear or hope to
see shaken in practice; which, in short (except perhaps
during some temporary crisis) was in the common esti-
mation placed *above* discussion. And the necessity of
this may easily be made evident. A state never is, nor,
until mankind are vastly improved, can hope to be, for
any long time exempt from internal dissension; for there
neither is nor has ever been any state of society in which
collisions did not occur between the immediate interests
and passions of powerful sections of the people. What,
then, enables society to weather these storms, and pass
through turbulent times without any permanent weakening
of the ties which hold it together? Precisely this—that
however important the interests about which men fall
out, the conflict does not affect the fundamental principles
of the system of social union which happens to exist;
nor threaten large portions of the community with the subversion of that on which they have built their calculations,
and with which their hopes and aims have become iden-
tified. But when the questioning of these fundamental
principles is (not an occasional disease, but) the habitual
condition of the body politic; and when all the violent
animosities are called forth, which spring naturally from
such a situation, the state is virtually in a position of
civil war: and can never long remain free from it in act
and fact."* Now, Mr. Jefferson's theory would keep society in a chronic state of chaos; by subjecting not laws,
measures, policy alone to the healthy revision of experience, but government itself, in all that should give the
sense of security and permanence, government in its very

---

* Mill's Logic, Book vi. chap. x. p. 582. American edition.

form and essence, its fundamental institutions—subjecting this to a periodical demolition by general consent, as the alternative of a violent revolution. It is impossible that society should exist upon such a basis. It is as if the citizens of New York should set apart certain periodical times hereafter for destroying their own houses, lest a mob should burn them down.

GOVERNMENT A NECESSITY.

Government, to answer properly its functions, must not only secure its subjects in their rights at home, and defend them abroad, but must carry the assurance of its own security and permanence. As Mill says, " there must be in the constitution of the state *something* which is settled, and not to be called in question." Now, to give this security, there must be in the minds of its citizens the conviction that GOVERNMENT is a Necessity of human Society, and therefore as really an ordinance of man's nature for his well-being, as any law or ordinance of the Creator concerning man. An absolute, independent individualism is impossible to a being who begins his existence under the restraints and obligations of the family, and who grows up amidst other families and persons, whose presence creates other mutual restraints and obligations. No man can assume this naked individualism as his stand-point of personal rights, and refuse allegiance to society except he can have in all things his own way. Society is not an aggregation of such units of individualism ; it is an organic whole, whose growth is parallel with the existence of mankind. " Man" says Montesquieu, " is born in society, and there he remains ;" always a member of it, and always having toward it relations and obligations which he did not create and cannot annul.

Society may be imperfect, corrupt, tyrannical in its spirit, its opinions, its laws; it may be arbitrary in its structure, unjust and exacting in its demands; the established order of things may demand renovation; yet the individual is not an independent force, outside of society, whose mission is antagonism and revolution, but a leavening power within society, of which he is an integral part.

The state inheres in society, and government is a prime necessity of its existence. Without government there is chaos and the mob. The government may be corrupt, unjust, oppressive; demanding reform even to the extent of revolution; yet men should be trained to the idea, not that they are born enemies of government, but that government, however needing to be rectified, exists as a necessity of their own existence.

This conviction, so opposite to Mr. Jefferson's theory of perpetual agitation at the very foundations of society, is justified alike by the teachings of Christianity, by a sound political philosophy, by the experience of mankind, and by common sense. And the education of the community in this view of government, as being *in its essence* an ordinance of the Creator for man's welfare, is a first step toward the stability of government. That is most stable which rests in the intelligent conviction of men that it is useful and necessary.

CONDITIONS OF STABILITY.

But this education should be furthered by the structure of the particular government commending itself to the confidence of its subjects as wise and just. It is necessary to its stability, therefore—

I. That government be founded in and for THE RIGHTS OF MEN, not in and for the interests of classes. I do not say that government shall not care for interests, since a large class of interests—the currency, the usages of contracts and inheritance, the code of commerce, the protection of authors and inventors, and the like—by common consent do fall within its province. But these are interests not so much of classes against classes, but of the whole community in and by its several members. By class interest we intend the special advantage of a section or caste in the community in opposition to the rest; as the interest of a ruling house or race, the interest of a nobility, of the priesthood, or of the army; or, as in some European cities of the Middle Ages, the interest of particular guilds, holding a monopoly of wealth, manufacture, trade. A government constructed with a view to conserve class interests, to favor the few at cost of the many, to uphold castes, political, ecclesiastical, hereditary, military, commercial—no matter in what interest—rests upon a false and therefore unstable foundation. For no caste-interest can be upheld by government save at the expense of some broad general right; and since all progress tends toward the assertion of human rights, and the abolition of class usurpations and wrongs, governments maintained in the interest of classes must sooner or later fall. But once a government is securely anchored in the rights of men, guarding the essential rights of human personality, and of liberty in the pursuit of good, and making these its just and equal care, it has in itself, and in its surroundings, the highest security and stability that can pertain to any human institution. And for this it is needful—

II. That society be organized in FREE INSTITUTIONS, which themselves are vital and permanent. The institution differs from the privilege or charter in that it is organic in society itself. When the confederate barons of England, with their retainers, drawn up in battle array at Runnymede, wrung from King John the Great Charter of June 19th, 1215, they gained certain concessions to personal liberty, which have ever since been held among the great prerogatives of Englishmen, *to wit:* local and open courts of justice, independent of fear or favor from the crown; and the pledge that no man should be arrested, imprisoned, fined, or otherwise injured in person or property, by act of the king himself, but only by the judgment of his peers, and by the law of the land. But these grand defences of liberty were held as concessions from the kingly power. They were written in the charter. They date from a parchment. Well, a hundred years before, Henry I. had given a charter of franchises, every copy of which he sought afterwards to destroy; and, four hundred years later, Sir Edward Coke could testify in Parliament that thirty-two times had the necessity arisen to have the provisions of Magna Charta solemnly reaffirmed and re-established against faithless kings. Such is the uncertain tenure of popular liberties when held as concessions from a superior power. Now, free and open courts in every county, a judiciary independent of the executive, the trial by jury for every accused person—these are no longer privileges, but rights; not concessions, but institutions. We do not go back to Runnymede for their origin; we do not search the musty parchments of Lincoln Cathedral and the British Museum for their sanction; they belong to the organic structure of our society; are a part of our growth—institutions that need not even a constitution to verify them.

The charter that Winthrop, with his rare eloquence, won from Charles II. for the colony of Connecticut, was so ample in the spirit of liberty, that after the Revolution Connecticut needed no enlargement of civil freedom to make her a true democracy. That charter, rescued from the grasp of a tyrannical governor, and hidden in the old Hartford oak, has survived both the colony and the oak, to see its ancient grants grown into the life of a State that no longer depends upon its favor; for the town meeting, the elective legislature, the home-made laws of each district and county, are institutions of the soil in which the people grow as the natural body of their political life. And so, when the free ballot, the free school, the free press, the independent judiciary, the local magistracy, have come to be institutions, each endowed with an organic life, then society itself is organized in the spirit of liberty, and liberty is safe, because it is no longer a grant from power, but itself the living, moulding Power in the state. This institutional form is a peculiarity of Anglo-Saxon liberty in distinction from the theoretical constitutions of the spasmodic republics of France. M. Ed. Laboulaye enumerates personal liberty, religious liberty, liberty of instruction, liberty of the press, municipal liberty, and liberty of association, as the natural and necessary concomitants of self-government; using the English term "self-government," and adding, "the word is lacking in French, because we have not the thing."* That is a thing of English growth, like the British oak that grows on through the ages, and outlives the storms.

III. To insure stability in government, THE GOVERNING POWER MUST FAIRLY REPRESENT THE WELFARE OF THE WHOLE PEOPLE. Founded in the rights of man and upon institutions of freedom, it must be the embodiment

* L'Etat et ses Limites, p. 72.

of the national good, so far as this is capable of being represented by official organs. The rulers therefore must be elective, and amenable to public opinion through the press and through the polls. Suffrage may be more or less limited, according to the dictates of experience—for it is yet an unsettled problem by what rule to adjust suffrage for the highest good of society as a whole; legislation may be divided in manner and responsibility, and representation may be direct or indirect, as is seen in our universal resort to two houses differently constituted;— but whatever these modifications of the elective principle, varying from the absolute democracy of a New England town meeting to the circuitous election of a United States senator, or the responsibility of a ministry appointed by the British crown to a negative vote of the House of Commons, still the principle must obtain that the government exists for the whole, and fairly represents the welfare of that whole. This is the essential conception of a free, popular government.

In such a conception, the principle of a political nationality, so much insisted on by European liberalists, finds its just weight. A nationality may be compounded of several races by intermarriage, within the same territorial limits, as is true to-day of the American people, the English, and, to some extent, of the French and the Italians. A nationality may also embrace within it races that remain physiologically distinct, while practically commingling as one people. Thus the negro and the Jew in this country retain their peculiarities of race, yet they do not exist apart as communities, but through the distribution of their individual members are integral parts of the nation. Entire homogeneousness of population, therefore, in respect of race and origin, is not essential to the unit of nationality, nor to secure an equal administration of the government for the whole people.

But where a race segregated territorially is joined politically to another race superior in numbers and power, as the Irish to the English, the Venetians to the Austrians, the Poles to the Russians; or where different races upon the same soil are kept collectively distinct by social and religious organization, like the Christian races in Turkey, there a proper and uniform sentiment of nationality is impossible, and there is a constant temptation for the larger and stronger race to govern the rest in its own interest. Hence, in order to a free popular government which shall consult the welfare of the whole people, the principle of nationality must enter fairly, though not exclusively, into the constitution of such a government.

Not nativism, in a narrow partisan sense, but nationality, as comprehending the whole people in one unit of political existence, is essential to our idea of a free popular state. There must be " a feeling of common interest among those who live under the same government, and are contained within the same natural or historical boundaries; so that they shall feel that they are one people; that their lot is cast together; that evil to any of their fellow-countrymen is evil to themselves; and that they cannot selfishly free themselves from their share of any common inconvenience by severing the connection."* In this sense of the term, a strong and active principle of nationality is essential to the durability of the body politic; and hence the government must be constituted and administered impartially, for the whole people.

* Mill's Logic, B. vi. chap. 10, p. 583.

A TRUE POPULAR SOVEREIGNTY.

At the first, as we have seen, popular liberties were concessions from the reigning power. Next these were secured by constitutional checks upon the royal prerogative, as when the British Commons carried the great point of originating money bills and voting subsidies to the crown. But government by the people is not fairly attained until the people, in distinction from any hereditary class among them, elect their rulers, and are themselves eligible to the place of power. Lord Brougham defines the essence of an aristocracy to be, that "a class should exist endowed with the supreme power, while into that class admission is denied to the people at large, or can be had only by consent of the select few." Now, to restrict suffrage by distinctions or limitations of blood, race, color, birth, or hereditary rank, would be to create an aristocracy of electors; but to attach to the right of suffrage certain conditions of age, residence, property, or education, does not create an aristocracy, since the conditions are such as all men may attain unto. They rest not upon natural differences, nor hereditary artificial distinctions, but upon personal merit.

So with qualifications for office. The state may require that, to be eligible to certain offices, one must be native born; that for others he must be of a certain age; that for certain posts in the army and navy he shall have graduated at the military or the naval school; but none of these conditions restrict the rights or the freedom of the citizen, or deprive him of his just weight in public affairs. So long as the people, in distinction from an hereditary family, and in distinction from an exclusive order of men in the community, are themselves the ultimate source of power, and, as a whole, do directly or indirectly participate in the supreme power of the state, there is a free popular government, whatever modifications expediency or experience may apply to the elective franchise or to the tenure of office.

With all his radical proclivities, Jefferson defines a government by the people to be that in which the choice of representatives is shared " by every man of ripe years and sane mind, who either contributes by his purse or person to the support of his country."* This definition can hardly be improved; yet it would disfranchise many who boast themselves the disciples of Jefferson, who in this hour of their country's need and peril contribute neither purse nor person to its support!

Aristotle would reduce all governments to two kinds, marked by opposite tendencies;—" that in which the good of the community is every thing, and that in which it goes for nothing." A free popular government, in which every thing tends normally to the good of the community, is the perfection of government, and has the highest warrant of stability.

NEED OF A CONSTITUTION.

IV. Yet it is needful that a free government be defined and regulated by a CONSTITUTION, itself amendable. The community, whose good is the end of government, does not always at the first discern its own good; does not always consult that good simply, or in the best manner; is not always free from prejudice or passion, from ignorance or party bias, or the influence of base and artful men: and therefore a free popular government needs checks upon itself, in the interest of both justice and

* Jefferson's Works, vol. vii. p. 319

liberty. Such a government can be safely administered only under a written constitution—the organic law of the state ; a constitution framed in a time of calmness, with wise deliberation, and for the one purpose of making the government to be administered under it, best subserve the welfare of the whole people. Not liberty alone, but "law-girt liberty ;" not mere popular government, but constitutional regulated freedom,—a government at once by law and under law ; and that law supreme and abso lute in its authority, yet itself restrained from an arbi trary and despotic infallibility because it is *amendable ;—* not however by the government nor by the populace, but by the solemn deliberative action of the chosen representatives of the sovereign power ; this union of LAW and LIBERTY, of free government with fixed authority, combines in the highest degree the stability of freedom with the flexibility of its forms—the order of society with the improvement of political administration. A government thus constituted can stand if human society can exist ; it is made to stand ; it ought to stand.

PERFECTION OF THE UNITED STATES GOVERNMENT.

Never before in the history of the world have these several elements of stability in government been combined as in the Government of these United States. Founded upon the broadest declaration of the essential equality and the inalienable rights of men; embosomed in organic institutions of justice and of freedom ; fairly representing the whole people, and constituted for their equal benefit ; and ordered by that grand Constitution, the elaborated, concentrated, and harmonious wisdom of the sages of the nation ; accepted by the people, and by them ordained " to establish justice, promote the general welfare, and secure the blessings of liberty to themselves and their posterity :"—a Constitution that denies to the ablest general or statesman a title of nobility ; that makes the President of the nation liable to impeachment for treason, bribery, or other high crimes and misdemeanors ; that forbids Congress to assume any powers not expressly delegated ; that watches and checks every tendency of government to encroach upon the people; and then says to the humblest citizen, in the name of the greatest of nations, " Your speech, your religion, your business, your locomotion shall be free; your person and your house shall be secure ; you shall not be deprived of life, liberty, or property, without due process of law ; if accused of crime, you shall have a speedy and public trial, by an impartial jury of your own district ; you can compel your witnesses, and shall have counsel at our cost for your defence. You—the individual man, down there in the most humble and obscure position in society—in the eye of the Constitution, are greater than all its official executors : them it watches and restrains, that they do you no wrong ; you it defends and secures in every right." Such a government is made to stand ; it ought to stand ; IT WILL STAND.

THE RIGHT OF REVOLUTION.

But how does such a government stand toward that right of revolution, which was never more strongly asserted than in its own origin ?

There *is* a right of revolution. The divine warrant for civil government, given both in the Bible and in the nature of things, cannot be pressed, as the dotard on the throne of Prussia would press it, into sanctioning tyranny, and forbidding the redress of wrongs by an appeal to arms. The right of resistance is, in its place, as sacred as the duty of obedience. The Bible, speaking in popular language, and not with the formal exactness of philosophical definition, lays down general truths broadly, without those qualifications and exceptions that specific cases would fairly authorize. The doctrine so clearly taught, that Christianity is not to organize a crusade against civil government, but should uphold the state as a necessary and a divine institution, proceeds on the assumption that the government, in the main, answers the purpose of its institution, as the protector of the good and a terror to the evil. If, however, by injustice and violence, the government becomes an unbearable oppression, there rests in *Society*, which gives form to the State, an ultimate right to redress itself, by overturning or otherwise changing the falsified government, in the interest of a true and righteous ordering of the state.

We are liable, however, to be misled by the term " *Right* of Revolution," as if this were a reserved right lodged somewhere within the political structure itself. But a revolution is the overturning of the established order of things with a view to establish a new order in its stead ; and therefore, in strict logic, there can be no right of revolution latent within an existing political system.

What we intend by the right of revolution may be better defined as the moral DUTY OF RESISTANCE to tyranny and wrong, even to the extent of breaking up the whole established order of things ;* not our right, then, as citizens or subjects, but our duty as men. And

* For this distinction I am indebted to my valued friend, Prof. Francis Lieber, LL.D.

this duty, when the case arises, we must be ready to perform, or, for example's sake, to perish in the attempt. But, as a duty, it must be capable of being defended upon moral grounds, defended before God, defended in history, defended by its motives and results.

To justify a revolution, therefore—to clothe it with the sanctity of duty—these three things must concur:

1. The movement must be founded in justice, and must aim at a result which in itself will be right and good.

2. The evils against which it protests must be grievous and unbearable wrongs.

3. The revolution should appear to be the only, and, at the same time, a feasible mode of redress.

Bad government, at the worst, may be better than anarchy;—and such are the horrors of civil war, that no community or portion of the body politic can be justified in invoking these, except as a last resort against desperate wrongs, and with a reasonable hope of success in the attempt to win justice by the sword. While, therefore, the right of revolution may be valid for Italy against Austria, or for Poland against Russia, it is impossible that a case should ever arise in which an armed insurrection against a constitutional free government would be justifiable. In such a government the Constitution stands ever to restrain, or, if need be, to judge the administrators of government in matters of alleged injustice; and the acting government itself can be changed at limited periods. All wrongs can be redressed, all wrongdoers can be removed in time, by peaceable methods; and, at the most, nothing could be gained by insurrection but a change of rulers—which can be gained without it —and an insurrection could give no better security for the character of those it raised to power than would a peaceable election.

THE RIGHT USE OF TERMS.

Let us look at this more closely. There is a right or duty of revolution. But what sort of a right is it? A constant, omnipresent right, that may be put forth at any time, for any end? Is it the right to get up a mob and a counter-mob, a barricade and a counter-barricade, at every election? Is it what the "New Gospel of Peace" describes as the specialty of a certain type of citizen, who "loveth fighting for fighting's sake, and without schyndees he pineth away, and life is a burden unto him?" The first French republican constitution had a section declaring that citizens have a right to resist with arms unjust laws. This Dr. Lieber well describes as "armed nullification *en permanence;*" or, we may say, Government holds only under a lease from Anarchy, voidable at will.

My neighbor has a right, *in extremis*, to blow up his house with gunpowder, to arrest the spread of fire. But is the right to put kegs of powder into his cellar and blow up his house, the same kind of a right with that to dig a cellar and build a house by my side? Clearly, this becomes a right only in a great emergency, when it is the last hope of deliverance; at any other time the act would be a crime. Now, the right of revolution is of that nature; it is not absolute, but conditional; only certain rare exigencies and combinations can bring it into being, and without these, clearly and forcibly existing, it is a crime to attempt a revolution.

So great are the calamities of civil war, so frightful the horrors of anarchy, that the overturning of government may be rightfully attempted only for the ends of justice

3*

—never for the interest of a party, for the success of a dynasty, from disappointed ambition, or for a mere change of political policy. There must be in it that which appeals to the moral sense of men as just and right, to warrant a movement that may deluge the land with blood and shroud every house in mourning.

And, even with right upon its side, the movement will not be justified by mere annoyances, discomforts, or occasional burdens and grievances, that affect not the core of society, and that time might relieve or allay, but by accumulated and unbearable wrongs.

And even then the revolution must have a fair prospect of success to warrant the fearful responsibility of attempting it. " The evils must have become intolerable before the resistance is to be attempted ; the parties whose rights are invaded must first exhaust every peaceful, and orderly, and lawful means of obtaining redress. An insurrection is only to be justified by the necessity which leaves no alternative ; and the probability of success is to be weighed, in order that a hopeless attempt may not involve the community in distress and confusion."*

EARL RUSSELL'S THREE REBELLIONS.

Each of the three rebellions cited by Earl Russell had these justifying grounds, that constituted it a rightful revolution. When the ill-fated Charles had arrested Parliamentary leaders for words uttered in debate ; had assessed money without law, and imprisoned citizens for non-payment ; had denied the writ of habeas corpus in time of peace ; had suppressed Parliament ; had used the Star Chamber for the torture of political victims, by branding, whipping, slitting the nose, cropping the ears,

* Brougham's Political Philosophy. Part iii. chap. xii.

at the tyrant's whim; and, finally, would turn the army into an engine of his despotic will, it was plain that all the rights and liberties of Englishmen were gone. These were unbearable wrongs. Begun under the despotic James, they had grown and multiplied, under his more despotic son, against laws and charters, against petitions and remonstrances, against oaths and covenants, against patience and concession, until the only hope of redress lay in an appeal to arms;—the only alternative of the nation was an unmitigated despotism or a violent revolution.

And when, forty years later, the bad blood of the Stuarts, not cured by the terrible lancet of Whitehall, broke out anew in the monstrous dogma of James II.—"the king from God—law from the king"—and every thing in the state—religion, trade, finance, justice, the persons and the lives of men—must be held at the absolute will of the tyrant, there was need that the unfinished revolution of the last generation should be completed by expelling the Stuart dynasty, and bringing in a new order of things. That last great appeal of Englishmen to the sword was for justice and the rights of man, against accumulated and unbearable wrongs; and well has it been said, that the English government was then "made to rest upon the people's Right of Resistance, as upon its cornerstone."

And with what solemn majesty did our fathers take up their reluctant appeal to arms. the last, only redress against unbearable wrongs! That long indictment against the king of Great Britain, of abuses and usurpations having in direct object the establishment of an absolute tyranny, were itself their sufficient justification. But they do not plead this until every moral means has been exhausted. "In every stage of these oppressions,

we have petitioned for redress in the most humble terms;
our repeated petitions have been answered only by repeated injuries." And so, acquiescing in the necessity,
they take up this last dread appeal to the Supreme
Judge of the world.

Proud are we to be the offspring of three such rebellions—conceived only in the interest of Justice, attempted only at the stern behest of duty to Liberty and to
Man, and achieved without abuse of power or stain of
crime. And therefore do we stand in the name of all
that these solemn ordeals of the sword have secured, to
insist that well-ordered freedom shall not be disturbed
by a factious insurrection mocking the sacred name of
revolution.

THE TEST APPLIED TO OUR OWN GOVERNMENT.

Test now the right of revolution by the principles of
a constitutional government founded in institutions of
popular liberty, and existing for the ends of justice, of
order, and of freedom. Against a government so constituted, in its structure, its genius, its aims, no plea of injustice or wrong can ever arise, no warrant for resistance
in the name of human rights, or for any real interest of
man. The utmost ground of complaint would lie against
the temporary administration of such a government—
the usurpation of power by those in authority, or the
tyranny of the majority in violation of the constitution,
or through a perversion of its forms. But this can never
go to such a pitch of unbearable outrage that the overturning of the state will be the only, and, therefore, the
justifiable remedy.

Under an autocracy, like that of Russia, either of two
things, or both, might be gained by a revolution:—a
change in the dynasty, or a change in the form of government, to a republic or a limited monarchy. Yet, under
such a government, revolution is not justified by every
wrong. If Nicholas is an oppressor, it may be well to
wait for Alexander. He may emancipate the serfs; he
may inaugurate a system of constitutional freedom. It
is yet to be proved whether Poland will now gain more
by fighting than might have been won by endurance.
There is reason to suspect that her present insurrection
was prompted by her aristocracy, in order to perpetuate
serfdom. Yet, for her accumulated wrongs, there does
remain to Poland the sacred right of revolution, in the
interest of nationality.

In a mixed government, like that of England, though
no change of form may be desirable, a revolution might
be needful to purge the land of a race of tyrants like the
Stuarts. Yet when a headstrong fool upon the throne
of Prussia attempts to subvert the constitution by royal
prerogative, it does not follow that revolution is the
remedy. Better than a deluge of fire and blood, the at-
titude of legal and moral resistance in which that nation
calmly waits for the accession of the Crown-Prince—
doubly pledged to freedom by his own professions, and
by the hand of England's noblest daughter.

But, under such a government as I have described, a
change in the form of government is in no case to be
desired, since such a change could only be a step back-
ward, against the rights and liberties of men. The form
of government, if not the best conceivable, is the best
attainable with human imperfection. The only thing to
be sought, therefore, by revolution, is a change of rulers

and measures. Grant, then, that these are wicked and oppressive in the extreme; that rulers sworn to uphold the Constitution violate it by outrages upon the conscience, the property, the person, the life of the citizen. Shall we seek redress by an armed revolution?

In taking up arms to oust an administration, we begin by violating the Constitution. Still, the exigency might allow for that. But if we triumph in the fight, what next? Shall the men raised into power by the bayonet be kept there by force of arms? Then do we trample free government under foot! Then do we substitute for a free election a war of factions, and inflict upon society a greater evil than we cure! Is there a man in all this land who would consent, upon the plea of "military necessity," that the present Administration should hold over without the form of a new election?

If, then, to save liberty, we fall back upon the election, the ousted party may renew its triumph at the polls; or what guarantee have we in history, or in human nature, or from our experience of politicians, that the very men we have fought into power will not turn and sell themselves to the conquered for their votes? Holding the form of free government to be the best, can any thing be hoped for by revolution under such a government that would warrant the effusion of treasure and blood, the monstrous cost and suffering and woe of civil war? —any thing that were not as surely gained by time and patient working?

I grant the immediate check to usurpation, by means of armed resistance, and the moral lesson of such resistance to wrong. But the government itself, remember, is constituted in and for right; and society, in the end, gravitates toward the right. At length reason and moral

firmness, with wise political action, must conquer abuse
and wrong in a free government. There is for these a
sure and peaceful remedy; and therefore, to stir the
foundations of society by revolt, and give the fatal precedent of fighting factions, is itself a wrong. The most
wayward and tyrannical majority may be subdued,
the most adroit political usurpation may be overcome
without recourse to arms. And such incidents of free
government can never be swept from our path by
revolution.

FREEDOM A MORAL REGULATOR.

I have assumed, as underlying this whole argument,
that in the condition of society essential to the origina-
tion of such a government, certain principles of human
nature, under the action of established moral causes, will
essentially secure the well-ordering of the state. This
is the safeguard against a permanent abuse of power by
the majority, and also against such an extreme and permanent corruption of the people as would vitiate their
-political institutions. I affirm neither the divine right
of republics nor the infallibility of the people; but, the
existence of free *institutions* at the basis of a popular
constitutional government, supplies a regulative power
against the misdirection of the government, and against
the abuse of popular sovereignty. Those institutions—
the free press, the free school, the free church, the local
administration of political affairs and of legal justice—
are training schools, both in personal liberty and in self-
government.

Freedom of individual pursuits favors business occu-
pations and domestic arrangements, that make the citi-

zen conservative of law and order, even upon selfish grounds. A man's family, his shop, his farm, are so many hostages for his loyalty to a state that is constituted upon the very principle of protecting him in their possession and use. The Red-republican, or socialist, of continental Europe, the ragged barn-burner of Tipperary—however at the first confounding liberty with lawlessness,—no sooner tastes the satisfaction of acquiring and owning property, than he becomes the champion of order. Freedom of discussion, sooner or later, exposes the arts of demagogues; freedom of personal action breaks the spell of parties, and fritters down majorities when these would grow tyrannical. A Van Buren, a Douglas, a Dickenson, will break the very organization they had helped to compact. A collective despotism is hard to maintain under the forms of free government, with a constitution pledged to liberty and justice, and with the oft-recurring scrutiny of the ballot-box. Indeed, against the dearest interests of individuals; against the vested rights of man in the organic structure of the state; against the power of knowledge, of virtue, of religion, in a free community, it is impossible that the despotism of a majority should stand long enough to warrant resistance by violence. This is emphatically true when, as in our government, the ruling power is not the naked numerical majority, but what Mr. Calhoun so aptly styled the CONCURRENT MAJORITY of two bodies representing different interests, parties, forms, or policies in the state. Seldom can this concurrent majority be held together for a wrong upon society itself. To resist by force a majority or a faction *forcefully subverting the government*, is not revolution, but the defence of order, freedom, and law.

A CASE IN POINT.

By a long-practised usurpation, and the corruption of a political majority, the slave aristocracy gained control of the Government of the United States; abrogated the ancient covenants of freedom; converted the Supreme Court into an agent of despotism; and made the Constitution itself, and all the machinery of government, the slave of slavery. We met that usurpation how? By organized violence? We met it first by moral resistance to the kidnapper's law, standing upon the indefeasible rights of conscience, which can never succumb to wrong. We harbored the fugitive and bore the penalty. We met that usurpation by argument and appeal to the judgment and the moral sense of the nation. We met it by political organization, and measures for self-protection and the defence of liberty. We met it by the steady growth of intelligence and virtue in public sentiment, waiting for a generation of young men who would not be slaves. And then, at last, we met it squarely in the issue of a Presidential election and triumphed over it, by lifting an honest and true man to the Executive chair. And now we see how, in all this, Divine Providence had worked with and for us, giving us in Mr. Lincoln, His chosen instrument for the salvation of the nation and the emancipation of a race. But there is no stain of blood upon our hands: there is no cry of widows and orphans in our ears; there is no line of graves across our path; there is no protest of outraged liberty and right against us, for that great moral and political revolution achieved by fidelity to truth and freedom, and by patient continuance in well-doing.

So will it ever be with the cause of Right under free

government. Nothing else ought to prevail, and this surely will prevail. Revolution for a wrong is a crime. Armed revolution for the right finds no justifying necessity; for I repeat it, that the government is already constituted for the Right; that society surely gravitates toward the Right; and that truth and reason will win the Right, unsullied by the smoke, the tears, the bloody anguish of war. Here, then, revolution can have no footing and no defence.

THE CRIME OF THE REBELLION.

It follows from these premises that the authors of this Southern rebellion are guilty of a stupendous and unmitigated CRIME—a crime that finds no specious precedent in the history of revolutions, and no pretence of authorization in any right of society or any philosophy of the state.

This rebellion is an armed assault upon the AUTHORITY OF THE GOVERNMENT as constituted by regular procedure, under the supreme organic law of our civil liberty. It is therefore an insurrection against the order of society, as here instituted and regulated by the spirit of freedom. It is impossible to evade this simple fact. There is but one lawful government possible in these United States. That government rests not upon a compact or confederation of independent sovereignties; but, after the failure of such confederation, the PEOPLE of the United States, in their original sovereignty, prescribed the mode of constituting and of renewing the government, and, if need be, of amending it. The insurrection is against GOVERNMENT as representing the organic order of a free society.

It is, therefore, an assault upon the SOVEREIGNTY OF

THE NATION, as expressed through its constitutional forms. For what is it that, in this country, is represented in the government? A family? a house? a tribe? a faction? Nay, the majestic Sovereignty of a Free People; and this the Rebellion would drag down and trample under foot.

The rebellion is an assault upon the PRINCIPLE OF REGULATED LIBERTY, which is the highest form of political freedom. For the ballot-box and the free popular election, it would substitute armed dictation at the polls, or a standing war of factions. Greater than all questions of public policy and of social economy arising out of the war, is this question of the ages: Shall a free people be governed by laws constitutionally enacted, or by the law of the strongest and the terror of the sword? The heirs of three revolutions that sprung out of that very question, now see all put in jeopardy that these revolutions had gained.

For, this rebellion is an assault upon ALL THE PRINCIPLES AND INSTITUTIONS OF JUSTICE, HUMANITY, AND FREEDOM embodied in our national life, and upon all the hopes combined with it. It is distinctly a war of civilizations, of systems of social order—a war of despotism, built upon the degradation of labor and of man, against freedom, with the school, the press, the ballot, the dignity of labor and of man. I put it to Earl Russell if it is a question, if it can be a question, whether such a rebellion is simply a great fact or a great crime? a crime of so deep a dye that a son of the English Revolution should spurn all relations with the people guilty of it. A greater Englishman than Russell, Mr. Richard Cobden, has said: "This is an aristocratic rebellion against democratic government."

THE GUILT OF ITS ABETTORS.

To palliate this rebellion, to apologize for its authors, is to invoke its guilt and to share its criminality. The issue it involves is in no sense a question of political measures, parties, or policy; no question of the modification of government for the welfare of the people, for any right of man, for any interest of justice or humanity. It is simply a crime against society, a crime against freedom, a crime against man. He who would wink at such a rebellion, who would openly or covertly further it, cannot be the friend of his country; cannot be the friend of its Constitution; cannot be the friend of liberty. He makes himself partaker in an enormous crime. To allow the rebellion is to warrant the subversion of free institutions by factious violence; to warrant an armed resistance to the constitutional judgment of the people. And that, if ever we are capable of it, will be the crime of national suicide, which God will surely visit upon us, and for which there will be no grave deep enough to hide our infamy.*

OUR DUTY TO MANKIND.

We are called upon, therefore, to annihilate this rebellion, in the interest not only of our social order, but of all mankind. Here at last the right of revolution, to which the groaning peoples of Europe cling, had wrought itself out in the highest forms of liberty attainable by man. Hungary, Venetia, Greece, Poland, France, how

---

* The allowance of a right of secession would be equivalent to self-destruction. As Laboulaye has said, "A federal contract which may be broken at the pleasure of the confederated states, carries anarchy and dissolution within itself, for it subsists only at the good-will of the parties, and is at the mercy of human passions."

terrible their penalties in abortive attempts to win popular freedom by revolution! How uncertain as yet the hold of Prussia, and even of Italy, upon constitutional rights so dearly won! Here alone was it seen that revolution in behalf of justice and freedom against unbearable tyranny, could issue in a wholesome, consistent, orderly, and stable Liberty. And now, the viperous despotism nursed upon our soil would smite that Liberty: and all the despots of the earth are crying, "Smite it down; let the people see what comes of their revolutions, and constitutions, and republics." We stand, then, for the suffering peoples of the earth, to prove that they suffer and rise and fight not for a mockery, but for a grand and imperishable reality; that Liberty once fairly won, and girded about with institutions of justice and freedom, can be shaken no more; can stand against foes without and foes within; stand in the might of Truth! stand in the heart of a Great People! stand in the strength of Almighty God!

We fight to-day for Poland, for Hungary, for Venice, putting down the crime of rebellion against Freedom, that their right of revolution for freedom may stand unimpeached by our failure,—may vindicate itself by the finality of our success.

THE HOPE OF THE WORLD.

How bright the future that shall dawn upon the world when this rebellion is effectually put down, and with it is put down forever the pretence of revolution against a free government! When we finish this war, we shall close that chapter of human history. That question settled, the political Millennium of mankind will have begun; the golden age of Reason and of Right. Brougham, in-

deed, has said, that " mixed governments can exist only
by keeping alive the right of resistance." That is their
affair who live under such a government. But I have
faith in a higher philosophy for the Republic, a nobler
future for man. I cannot think that human society was
meant to rest upon a volcano, and to rock alternately
from despotism to civil war. I cannot think that LIBERTY
must forever maintain a struggle for existence. Nay, the
very right of resistance from which it sprang, shall one
day cease because all other rights are gained. The sub-
terranean mutterings of revolution shall be hushed in
the grand organ-swell of freedom and righteousness that
shakes the earth and fills the sky.

Then Peace shall be no more a sentiment upon the
lips of Philanthropy, but the normal condition of a State
that has within it no disturbing cause—of a World that
acknowledges justice and freedom to be established
against all pretence of revolution. Then war, seen to be
hopeless in the cause of wrong, shall no more be de-
manded by the stern necessity of right. Far transcend-
ing the material prosperity and grandeur that we look
for, after the war, will be the triumph of these great
ideas :—that Liberty extinguishes the right of revolution
by securing all the rights of man, and that it tramples
out Rebellion in the name and the hope of humanity.
" Then shall the land be filled with judgment and righteousness, and wisdom and knowledge shall be the stability of our times." May I but see the dawning of that
day, when these blood-dripping clouds are overpast, and
though, to further it in my poor measure, I should even
go down childless to the grave, I will bless God to
leave to an unknown posterity the golden heritage wrung
from the mortal agony of this sublime, decisive hour!

www.ingramcontent.com/pod-product-compliance
Lightning Source LLC
Chambersburg PA
CBHW030908260626
47169CB00008B/2751